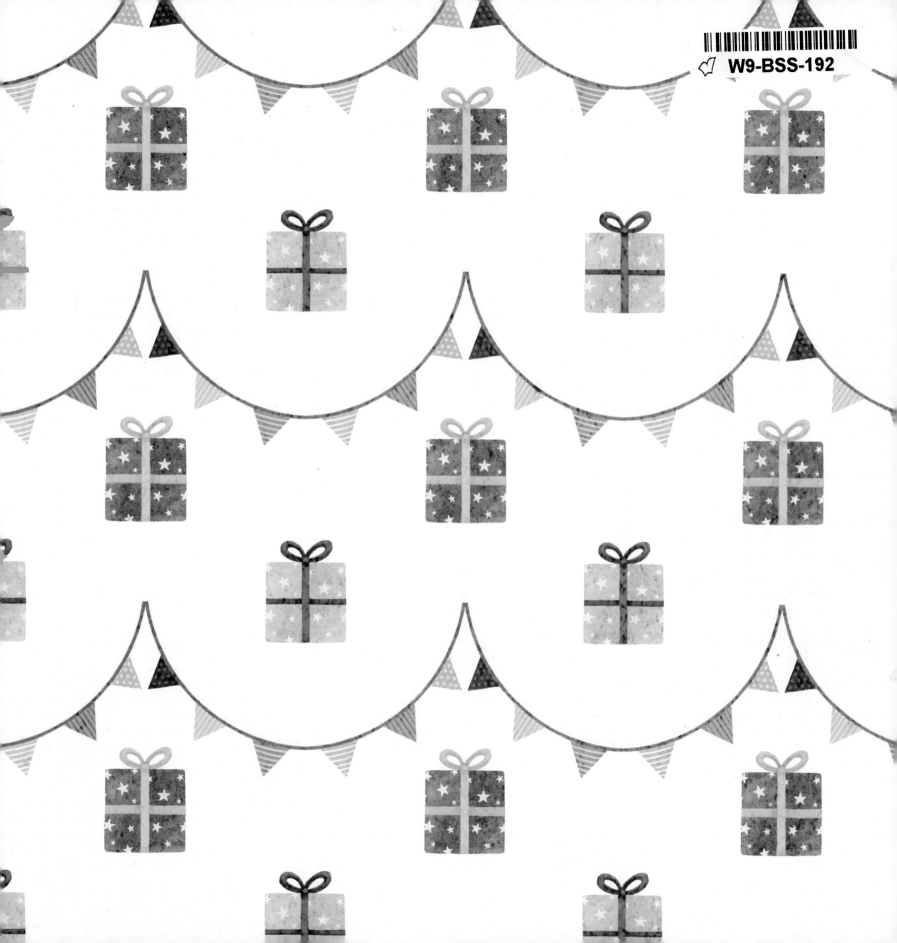

For Eliza Hayes

STERLING CHILDREN'S BOOKS
New York

An Imprint of Sterling Publishing
1166 Avenue of the Americas
New York, NY 10036

First Sterling edition published in 2016.

Originally published in 2015 in Great Britain by
Macmillan Children's Books
a division of Macmillan Publishers Limited
20 New Wharf Road, London N1 9RR
Basingstoke and Oxford
Associated companies throughout the world
www.panmacmillan.com

ISBN 978-1-4549-1846-2

For information about custom editions, special sales, and premium and corporate purchases,
please contact Sterling Special Sales at 800-805-5489 or specialsales@sterlingpublishing.com.

Manufactured in China
Lot #:
2 4 6 8 10 9 7 5 3 1
03/16

www.sterlingpublishing.com

The Best Birthday Present Ever!

Ben Mantle

STERLING CHILDREN'S BOOKS
New York

Squirrel was super excited! He'd been invited to a party.
But not just any party, it was . . .

Big Bear's Birthday Bonanza!

Now he needed to find a birthday present for his best friend, Bear.

Bear already had lots
of bubble bath,

and he definitely didn't
need any slippers.

All the animals went
to the toy store.
But Squirrel wanted to
get something different.

WOODLAND
TOY STORE

Suddenly he was struck by a *brilliant* idea!
He would give Bear . . .

A stick! He scoured every tree looking for the perfect one.
But they were all . . .

too heavy,

too leafy,

or too wriggly.

Squirrel was about to give up his search
when he tripped over something . . .

It wasn't too
heavy or leafy,
and it certainly
wasn't alive.

"Bear will love it!"
he shouted.

Squirrel rushed straight home to wrap the stick.

Bear would never guess what it was now.

To make it even more special, he tied a big bow around it.

This was going to be the best birthday present *ever!*

It was the day of Big Bear's Birthday Bonanza.

"Happy birthday, Bear!" shouted Squirrel.
"I think you'll like your present."

It did look a lot smaller than the other gifts.
But Squirrel wasn't worried.

Everyone had so much fun at the party.
They danced, played games, and ate lots of cake.
Soon it was time to open the presents.

Bear picked up the largest present first and read
the label. *"To Bear from Rabbit."*
He tore off the paper.

"WOW! The Mallow O' Matic 5000 Marshmallow Cannon!"
gasped Bear. "Thanks, Rabbit."

Bear excitedly unwrapped more presents, each one getting better and better . . .

TURBO X FISHING ROD

from Fox

Thunder Boom Drum Kit

from Owl

Amazing
Pop-Up
Castle Tent

Looks Like
A House With
Two Floors!

FROM BADGER

"What great gifts!" he squealed.
Squirrel started to worry.

There was just one present left to open.

"I hope you like it," Squirrel whispered nervously.

Bear examined the gift carefully, wondering what it could be. He ripped off the paper.

"OH!" exclaimed Bear, staring at the stick in surprise.

"It's just what I've *always* wanted!" he said.
"Oh, thank you, Squirrel."

Everyone wanted to take a look at the stick.

"It's very small," said Owl.

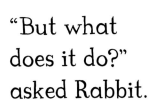

"How unusual!"
squeaked Mouse.

"But what
does it do?"
asked Rabbit.

"A stick this perfect can do absolutely *anything!*"
replied Bear. And he was right.

That week Bear and Squirrel spent all their time
playing with the stick.

It made an excellent
marshmallow fork,

they caught twice
as many fish,

and they made double
the noise on the drums.

They even flew
their very
own flag on
their castle.

But there was another game they liked to play even more . . .

Poking things.

They poked
squelchy things,

d e e p things,

and *floaty* things.

When they came across
a mysterious hole, they
poked it to see what
was inside . . .

SQUAWK!

The stick fell
to the ground
with a

SNAP!

"Oh, my lovely stick!" cried Bear.

"We'll never find another one as perfect as that," sighed Squirrel.

As they stared sadly at the two pieces, Bear realized something. Maybe it didn't matter that the stick was broken . . .

Because now they had the
TWO best birthday presents ever.